About This Book

Title: *Goal!*

Step: 5

Word Count: 203

Skills in Focus: All long vowel teams

Tricky Words: want, together, player, football, soccer, ball, basketball, score

Ideas For Using This Book

Before Reading:
- **Comprehension:** Look at the title and cover image together. Ask readers what they already know about team sports such as football and hockey. What new things do they think they might learn in this book?
- **Accuracy:** Practice saying the tricky words listed on page 1.
- **Phonics:** Tell students they will read words with long vowel teams. Explain that *ee, ea,* and *ey* can all make the long vowel sound /e/. The vowel team *oa* makes the long vowel sound /o/. Both *ai* and *ay* make the long vowel sound /a/. Have students look at the title of this book, *Goal!* Ask readers to point to the vowel pairing in the word. Help them practice blending the sounds in *goal*.

During Reading:
- Have readers point under each word as they read it.
- **Decoding:** If readers are stuck on a word, help them say each sound and blend the sounds together smoothly. Be sure to point out words with vowel teams as they appear. Briefly explain that the word *head* includes the *ea* vowel team but is pronounced with a short vowel /e/ sound.
- **Comprehension:** Invite readers to talk about new things they are learning about team sports while reading. What are they learning that they didn't know before?

After Reading:
Discuss the book. Some ideas for questions:
- How do players work together to score goals?
- What sports have you played before? What new sports would you like to try?

Sports teams want to score goals so they can win games.

Goal!

Text by Marley Richmond

Reading Consultant
Deborah MacPhee, PhD
Professor, School of Teaching and Learning
Illinois State University

PICTURE WINDOW BOOKS
a capstone imprint

Kids must play as a team so they can score.

Coaches teach kids how to play as a team.

Hockey

Kids play ice hockey as a team.

Each team has six players on the ice.

Pass the puck to help your team score a goal!

One player keeps the puck out of the goal.

Football
Kids play football on grass.

The team lines up on the field.

One player passes.

A teammate catches and runs up the field to the end zone.

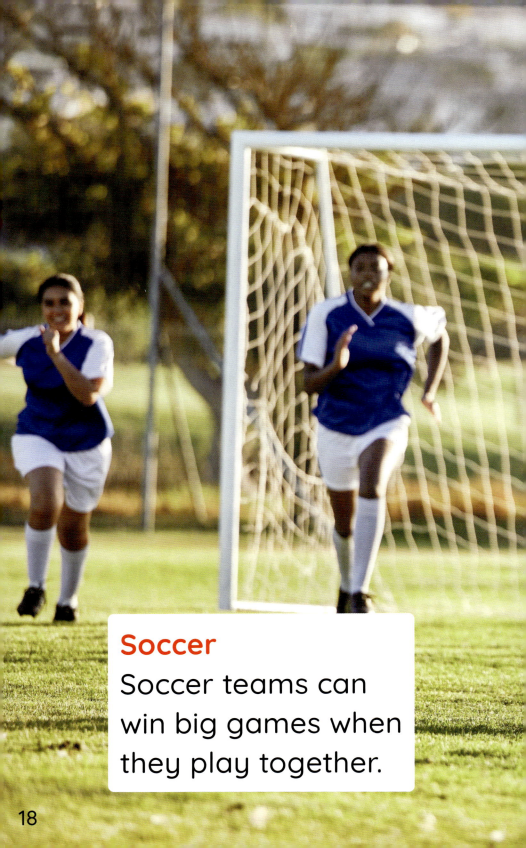

Soccer

Soccer teams can win big games when they play together.

Teams try to steal the ball to score goals.

Pass to your teammate on the field.

You can pass with your feet or pass with your head.

Kick the ball into the goal to score for your team!

Basketball
Kids play basketball on teams.

Each team has at least five kids.

Set up a screen to block the other team.

Pass, shoot at the net, and score!

A coach asks for a timeout.

28

She makes a plan to win with the team.

The key to win a game is to play as a team. Teamwork helps kids score goals!

More Ideas:

Phonics Activity

Matching Vowel Teams:
Prepare word cards with vowel teams. Words could include *ee, ea, ey,* or *oa*. Place the cards on a workspace. Ask readers to make pairs of words that use the same vowel team. Have readers sound out each pair of words and compare the long vowel sounds each vowel team makes.

Suggested words:
- *ee*: feet, keep, screen
- *ea*: team, teach, each, steal, least
- *ey*: hockey, key
- *oa*: goal, coach

Extended Learning Activity

Play as a Team:
Ask players to count from one to ten (or the number of readers in the group) with each player saying one number. If two players talk at the same time, the group must start over. Once the group counts to ten, ask readers to write about the game. Readers can describe how they worked as a team to meet a goal. Challenge readers to use words with vowel teams such as *ea, oa,* and *ay*.

Published by Picture Window Books, an imprint of Capstone
1710 Roe Crest Drive, North Mankato, Minnesota 56003
capstonepub.com

Copyright © 2026 by Capstone.
All rights reserved. No part of this publication may be reproduced in whole or in part, or stored in a retrieval system, or transmitted in any form or by any means, electronic, mechanical, photocopying, recording, or otherwise, without written permission of the publisher.

Library of Congress Cataloging-in-Publication Data is available on the Library of Congress website.

ISBN: 9798875227172 (hardback)
ISBN: 9798875230783 (paperback)
ISBN: 9798875230769 (eBook PDF)

Image Credits: iStock: AzmanJaka, 22–23, Digitalmediapro, 20, EHStock, 21, FatCamera, cover, 4, 6–7, 24–25, 32, groveb, 14–15, Ideas_Studio, 8–9, kali9, 5, 28–29, LightFieldStudios, 17, Portra, 30, SDI Productions, 16, SerrNovik, 26–27; Shutterstock: DardaInna, 1, 10–11, Lorraine Swanson, 12–13, Natee K Jindakum, 2–3, PeopleImages.com - Yuri A, 18–19

Printed and bound in China. 6274